Published in Canada by Inhabit Media Inc.
(www.inhabitmedia.com)

Inhabit Media Inc. (Iqaluit), P.O. Box 11125, Iqaluit, Nunavut, X0A 1H0
Inhabit Media Inc. (Toronto), 146A Orchard View Blvd., Toronto, Ontario, M4R 1C3

Design and layout copyright © 2015 Inhabit Media Inc.
Text copyright © 2015 by Neil Christopher
Illustration by Larry MacDougall copyright © 2015 by Inhabit Media Inc.

We acknowledge the support of the Canada Council for the Arts for our publishing program.

We acknowledge the support of the Government of Canada through the Department of Canadian Heritage Canada Book Fund program.

Printed and bound in Canada

Library and Archives Canada Cataloguing in Publication

Christopher, Neil, 1972-
[Stories of the amautalik]
    The dreaded ogress of the tundra / gathered and retold by Neil
Christopher ; illustrated by Larry MacDougall.

ISBN 978-1-927095-79-9 (bound)

    1. Inuit--Folklore. 2. Legends--Arctic regions. I. MacDougall,
Larry, illustrator II. Title. III. Title: Stories of the amautalik.

E99.E7C54613 2014   j398.2089'9712   C2014-907018-7

THE DREADED OGRESS OF THE TUNDRA

Gathered and Retold by
Neil Christopher

Illustrated by
Larry MacDougall

Inhabit Media
Iqaluit • Toronto

Dedication

This book is for Mia-Laure, and all the other little monsters that make life so much more interesting.

Contents

"The amautalik is an ogress who is hated and feared beyond all the other earth spirits. The naughtiest children can be made to stop crying and be silent at the mere mention of her name . . ."

Introduction

The Arctic can be a dangerous place. In the winter we have extreme cold and vicious winds. The sea ice can be unpredictable. And the long nights can make life difficult. But the Arctic has other dangers that are unknown to outsiders. One of these dangers has a name—*amautalik.* This word can strike fear into the hearts of all who recognize this name. The amautalik is a huge and powerful ogress. Inuit storytellers know many tales of strange beings who prey on children and lone travellers, but the amautalik is perhaps the most feared. Although this being's presence is felt across the circumpolar North, the Inuit that live inland, far from the coastal areas, seem to be the most familiar with this dangerous ogress.

Amautalik: Pronounced "a-mow-ta-lick."

An amautalik's basket is made from driftwood, sinew, bones, antlers, and anything else she finds.

The inside of the amautalik's basket is stuffed with rotting seaweed. And giant insects make a home in this decaying vegetation.

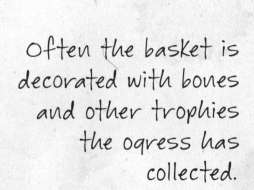

An amautalik is usually described as a huge, ugly woman who carries a large basket on her back. Sometimes, instead of carrying a basket, this ogress wears a huge *amauti* 🐦 made of walrus hide and lined with rancid seaweed.

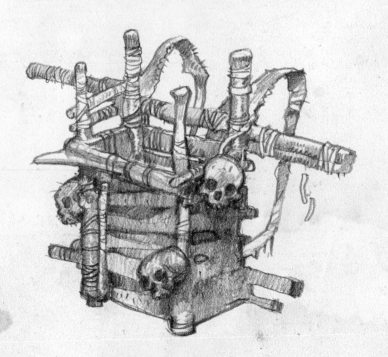

Often the basket is decorated with bones and other trophies the ogress has collected.

🐦 *Amauti*: A woman's jacket with a pouch used to carry children. Pronounced "a-mow-tee."

Although she may appear to be a heavy-footed, lumbering creature, an amautalik can move very quickly over the tundra.

This ogress
is happiest when
a child is trapped
in her basket.

Amautaliit 🐦 are primarily child-snatchers, but if they are hungry enough, they have been known to catch adults and carry them off as well.

🐦 *Amautaliit*: Plural form of amautalik. Pronounced "a-mow-ta-leet."

Amautaliit live underground. Due to the time an amautalik spends underground in her dwelling, you will usually find lichen, grasses, and dirt covering the ogress's hair and clothing.

The entrance to an amautalik's dwelling is usually littered with bones, both animal and human.

It is also said that amautaliit usually live underground and that once they have captured someone, they carry their captive back to an underground lair. Amautaliit usually have soil and plants matted in their hair and clothing, due to their life underground.

Often an amautalik's victims do not realize that they are being hunted until it is too late. This is probably because of the creature's ability to move silently over the rocky tundra. Despite the amautaliit's great size, strength, and stealth, many of the stories about them suggest that they have a weakness. It seems that the amautalik is not very intelligent and can be tricked or frightened away.

Although these ogresses are described differently in each region of the Arctic, they all have some unmistakable similarities. The most obvious (and the most frightening) is their desire to steal human children . . . for amusement . . . or food.

Welcome to the hidden world of the amautalik!

The Stories of the Amautalik

Stories of amautaliit can be found across the Canadian Arctic. Inuit oral history suggests that all regions of the North have been terrorized by these ogresses at one time or another.

In the following pages you will read stories from two different regions in the Arctic.

The Hungry Amautalik
& the Restless Children

In years past, Inuit families would sometimes gather to have song festivals. These festivals were a chance for people to get together to sing, dance, play games, and forget about hardships.

Many years ago, after a particularly long, dark, and cold winter, the weary people of a small village decided that they needed to raise everyone's spirits. So, in the spring, once the snow had begun to disappear, they held a huge song festival to celebrate the arrival of warmer weather. During the great festival, people sang songs, told stories, played games, and competed against each other in various activities.

After many days of fun and competition, the festival finished. The exhausted participants and spectators retired to their tents, just as the sun was peeking over the horizon. Soon, everyone in the village was asleep. Everyone, except for three restless children who did not want the festival to end.

They had stayed outside to play with some rope that was left behind from one of the sporting competitions. Two boys, Alliq🕊 and Makpalu,🕊 were trying to yank the rope out of each other's hands. Alliq, the older and larger boy, always won. Makpalu was not strong enough to pull the rope out of his friend's hand.

Kunaju,🕊 one of the smallest girls in the village, watched the two boys pull the rope back and forth. The morning sun made her squint, but Kunaju appreciated its warmth. She should have been in her grandmother's tent. She should have been sleeping, like almost everyone else in the village. Kunaju had not been sleeping well lately. The festival had been a welcome distraction for her, but now it was over and her worries had returned. Kunaju's mother had become very sick during the winter. Over a month ago, Kunaju's father had taken her mother by dog team to find a healer. Although her father had reassured her that everything was going to be fine, Kunaju was afraid that she might never see her mother again.

Unfortunately for Kunaju, Makpalu and Alliq were becoming bored with their rope game. Makpalu's hands were sore and Alliq was tired of winning all the time. A mean smirk slowly spread across Alliq's face as he decided to play one of his favourite games—bullying smaller children.

🕊 Alliq: Pronounced "al-lik."   🕊 Makpalu: Pronounced "mak-pa-loo."

🕊 Kunaju: Pronounced "koo-na-yoo."

Without warning, Alliq walked over to Kunaju and pushed her to the ground.

"Ouch! What was that for?" Kunaju complained.

Makpalu laughed, "Don't let her up. Babies should stay on the ground."

Just as Kunaju was trying to get up, Alliq walked over and pushed her back down.

"Stop it! Leave me alone!" Kunaju was trying to hold back the tears that were gathering behind her eyes.

Normally, an adult would have heard Kunaju's complaints and scolded the boys. But today, all the adults were sleeping deeply and could not hear the little girl's words. Alliq knew that he would not be stopped by by anyone and continued teasing the little girl.

This was a bad day to be without the supervision of the village adults. On this very same morning, an amautalik was travelling near the village looking for food. Kunaju's cries had caught the ogress's attention. Hungry and tired, the ogress decided to follow the sound, hoping it would lead her to something she could catch and eat.

From far away, the huge creature spotted the three children. The amautalik's eyes widened and she began to growl with excitement. She had not eaten in many days, and the sight of the children playing was making her mouth water. So, the ogress crouched down and crept behind a large rock.

Once safely hidden, the ogress peeked over the boulder to examine the village. To her surprise, the ogress could not see any adults watching over the children. The hungry amautalik smiled a huge, ugly smile and sank back down behind the rock.

"Children! . . . Slow-moving, fat, little children!
I will catch you!" the ogress whispered to herself.

Resting her chin on the rough surface
of the rock, the amautalik began to plan
her hunt. Because the children
were alone, she decided
to do what she did
best—run up and
grab them from
behind. Then
she would
carry them far
away so their
yells for help
could not be

heard by anyone in the village.

The amautalik leapt over the boulder and sprinted towards the children. Her huge strides moved her quickly over the tundra. As the ogress got closer, she could hear the children laughing and carrying on, oblivious to her rapid approach. The sound of careless children put an even larger smile on the ogress's face. She growled and increased her pace, springing easily over the rocks and loose terrain.

Alliq and Makpalu, not realizing that they were being hunted, continued their game of bullying Kunaju.

"Let's see the orphan cry some more," Alliq laughed.

"Stop saying that!" Kunaju demanded. "I am not an orphan."

Alliq and Makpalu had been teasing Kunaju about her parents for the last few weeks. They had told the other children that Kunaju's parents were tired of her and would never come back. They said she was an orphan now and had no one to protect her.

Kunaju knew the boys were wrong. She knew her mother and father loved her. They had not wanted to leave her, but her mother had been very sick. They promised to return as soon as they could. Kunaju's mother had even given her a special amulet to protect her while they were away. Her mother told her that the amulet was very old and had been made by her great-grandfather, who was a powerful *angakkuq*.🕊

"My parents promised to return," Kunaju said through her tears. "They even gave me a magic amulet for protection."

Both of the boys stopped laughing and stared at her. They could not believe what they had just heard.

"You think the amulet your mom gave you is magic? It looks like a bunch of old feathers tied with cord!" Alliq teased.

"You are sillier than we thought," Makpalu added. And with that, the two boys began to laugh even louder than before.

Alliq was the crueller of the two boys. His father was unkind to him, and in turn, Alliq was a bully to all the smaller children of the village. Alliq stopped laughing and glared at Kunaju. He slowly picked up a rock from the ground. He aimed it at Kunaju and teased, "Let's see if your magic amulet protects you from a simple rock!"

"Don't, Alliq! Please don't!" Kunaju pleaded

Alliq smiled, took aim, and drew his arm back. But before he could throw the rock at Kunaju, a large hand grabbed him by the hair

🕊 *Angakkuq*: A shaman. Pronounced "an-ga-kook."

and yanked him backwards.
"AAAaaaaahhhh!" he screamed as
he flipped upwards through the
air and came down hard in
a nest of rotten seaweed
and driftwood. He landed
so hard that all of the air was
knocked out of his lungs. He tried
to yell for help, but he could not
breathe. All he could do was
lie on his back in the foul-
smelling seaweed and
gasp for air.

Makpalu
and Kunaju
froze. They could
feel their hearts
pounding in their
chests. Each child's eyes slowly
crept up the ogress's body.
Neither child had ever seen a
being so large, or so frightening.

Their eyes climbed up and up until finally they were looking into the amautalik's ancient face. This huge woman was old, *really* old. Her skin was like walrus hide, with deep cracks and creases. Her hair was long and matted, as if it had never been brushed. The children could feel her hot breath on them as she growled. She smelled of old meat and rotting seaweed. As she opened her mouth to smile at them, they saw her teeth, which were yellow and rotten.

Before Alliq and Kunaju could scream, the ogress lunged towards them and grabbed them by their hair. Without much effort, the ogress lifted the children and flipped them into the basket. Makpalu and Kunaju landed on top of Alliq, just as he was catching his breath. The impact of the two children upon him caused Alliq to gasp for air once again.

The children, now tangled in the smelly seaweed, felt the ogress lurch forwards and begin to move. The amautalik sprinted over the land. Her huge strides carried them through rocky fields of grasses and flowers, across flowing streams, and over windswept, rocky hills. She was taking the captive children to her lair, far away from the village.

Kunaju was the first to free herself from the seaweed. She jumped to her feet and tried to climb out of the basket. But the basket was deep and the driftwood was slippery. The rough bounce of the amautalik's gait caused Kunaju to lose her footing and fall back on top of the squirming boys.

"Kunaju, help me! I can't get untangled," Makpalu pleaded.

"Help yourself," Kunaju answered as she stepped onto his head in another attempt to climb out of the basket. This time, as she grabbed hold of the twisted driftwood, she dug her nails into the slippery surface. With a firm grip of the basket, Kunaju was able to peek out over the ogress's head.

"HELP! HELP!" Kunaju shouted as loudly as she could. "Please help us!" She knew they were in trouble and that if she did not find help soon, she might never see her parents again.

The two boys, still tangled in the slippery seaweed, joined Kunaju in calling out for help. Alliq and Makpalu screamed the names of their parents, pleading for them to come and help. But it was too late. The creature had moved with such speed and power that they were already too far away from the village for their calls to be heard.

Kunaju realized that screaming was useless. She was the only one who could see how far the amautalik had travelled. She stopped yelling and turned her attention to the frantic boys tangled below her.

"Calm down. Be quiet!" Kunaju commanded. She reached down and began to help free them from the slimy strands of seaweed. The rotting ocean plants felt slippery in her hands and smelled worse than anything she could think of. She fought back the horrible feeling in her stomach and continued to untangle Alliq and Makpalu.

"Get this stuff off me, Kunaju. It smells awful and I think there are maggots crawling around the bottom!" Alliq shrieked.

"Quiet, Alliq. I will get you out. Just stop struggling," replied Kunaju in a stern voice.

She looked down at the bottom of the basket to see what Alliq was complaining about. He was right. There were fat maggots and large bugs crawling all over the seaweed. As Kunaju looked closer, she saw that both of the boys were now covered with squirming insects. Kunaju shivered with disgust and considered dropping the seaweed and climbing back up the basket. Instead, she took a deep breath and continued to help Alliq and Makpalu.

"Thanks, Kunaju," said Alliq.

"Yeah, thanks," repeated Makpalu. Kunaju just nodded and stared at the creatures crawling all over the heads and shoulders of the two boys.

"I think there is something in your hair," Kunaju said, tentatively.

"What? Where?" Alliq asked. Alliq looked over towards Makpalu, who was pointing at Alliq's head.

"What is that?" Makpalu demanded.

"You have bugs ALL OVER YOUR HEAD!" Alliq yelled back at Makpalu.

Instantly, the two boys lost whatever self-control they had and started bouncing around and slapping their heads, arms, shoulders, and any other parts of their bodies they could reach.

"Stop it! Stop it now!" Kunaju demanded. "We have to try to climb out of here. The bugs can wait."

The boys were not listening. With each slap, they could feel insects scurrying under their hands. Some of the softer-bodied insects squished and exploded with the force of their slaps, but the giant lice just hissed and squirmed deeper into the boys' clothing and hair. Alliq could feel the large insects crawling under his clothing.

He had heard what Kunaju said, but he could not stop trying to get the bugs off of him. Makpalu was in a state of panic as well. He could not hear Kunaju's voice over his own squealing.

Suddenly, the amautalik stopped. The children lost their balance and fell back into the decaying seaweed and insects. They scrambled all over each other, trying to get to their feet.

The amautalik,
now breathing hard
from her run, tilted
her head back and
sniffed the air. The
mixture of the
children's scent and
the putrid seaweed
smelled delicious to
her. The huge ogress
reached backwards into
her basket and grabbed
Kunaju by the hair. The
powerful ogress lifted
the small girl out of the
basket. Kunaju screamed
at the sting of being pulled
by her hair. She struggled
and struggled, but she
couldn't break the
ogress's grip.

Kunaju found herself dangling in front of the amautalik's leathery face. The ancient ogress looked over the meal she had caught for herself. Kunaju felt helpless. Her hair was twisted around the amautalik's clenched fingers, and nothing could make the ogress's powerful hands open.

"Let go of me!" Kunaju yelled. "Why have you taken us?" A throaty giggle was the ogress's only response. Kunaju's little hands began to scratch at the massive fingers of her captor, but, again, it was no use. As Kunaju was struggling, she felt the creature's foul breath. Once again, Kunaju twisted her body and swung in a frantic attempt to break the ogress's grip. The amautalik smiled with amusement at this little child's attempt to break free. Then the huge woman's nose wrinkled as she inhaled and slowly licked her lips. And suddenly, without warning, the ogress released her grip and dropped Kunaju to the ground.

THUD! Kunaju landed hard. She rolled to the side and tried to scramble to her feet, but the ogress stepped towards her, and with one of her huge feet, she pinned Kunaju to the ground.

Then the ogress removed the boys, one at a time, and repeated her close examination. She sniffed each boy carefully before she dropped him to the ground next to Kunaju. As they landed, the amautalik shifted her huge foot to ensure that each child was restrained beneath it.

After the children were inspected, the ogress smiled, licked her lips once more, and said in a deep, gruff voice, "You, small and fat. You smell tasty."

Then she took the skin belt from her jacket and wrapped it around the three squirming children. She pulled the belt tight, binding them together. The captives tried to wriggle away from the huge old woman. But struggling was useless.

When the amautalik was sure that the children were securely tied, she turned and stomped over to a large hole in the ground. This hole was the entrance to the amautalik's lair. The children had not noticed the hole earlier because it was half-hidden by rocks and vegetation. But as they began to look around, they spotted many bones scattered close to the hole. Kunaju quickly surveyed the remains that littered the ground. She realized that the remains scattered around this hole were not from animals. They were the weathered bones of unfortunate children.

"We've got to get out of here," Kunaju whispered to the struggling boys. "This creature is going to eat us."

Both of the boys stopped moving and looked at what Kunaju was staring at. The sight of human bones made Alliq and Makpalu start to cry.

"Please let us go!" Alliq screamed.

"Don't hurt us," Makpalu pleaded.

The amautalik glanced back at her captives and smiled. Her eyes were wide and saliva dripped from her mouth onto her chin.

"Fat little *qa'tava*.🦢 Me very hungry," replied the excited creature.

Before the amautalik disappeared down the hole, she smiled once again and said, "Me get my *ulu*.🦢" She then turned, and with a growl, climbed down the hole to fetch the cutting tool she needed.

The children were terrified. They struggled and struggled, but the rope just seemed to get tighter. Out of the corner of her eye, Kunaju noticed that the ancient amulet, given to her by her mother for protection, seemed to be twitching. She strained her neck to get a better look.

🦢 *Qa'tava*: The word for children in the language of the amautaliit. Pronounced "ka-ta-va."

🦢 *Ulu*: A woman's curved knife. Pronounced "oo-loo."

However, when she looked directly at the amulet, it wasn't moving at all.

"I must have imagined it," Kunaju thought to herself.

"What're we going to do?" sobbed Alliq. "I don't want to be eaten."

"Aaa . . . waaahhh . . . taagooo . . . haaammm," Makpalu blubbered. Makpalu was crying so hard that neither Alliq or Kunaju could understand what he was trying to say.

Kunaju was about to say something to Makpalu, when she felt the amulet twitch again. This time, when she looked down, the amulet continued to wiggle and move about. Kunaju then remembered what her mother had told her about the amulet. Kunaju tilted her head forward to get as close to the amulet as she could.

With her voice shaking, she whispered, "Help us get free."

The amulet stopped moving.

Kunaju whispered once again. "Please, help us."

Then the amulet began to twitch again. Its movements became more and more violent, until finally it broke free of the cord and fell onto the ground.

Kunaju watched in amazement as the old amulet made of feathers and sinew suddenly sprouted wings and legs. Slowly, some of the feathers formed a little head with a small yellow beak. The old amulet had turned into a bird—a little snow bunting!

Both Alliq and Makpalu stared at the snow bunting in silence. They could not believe what they had just seen.

"Did . . . did that amulet just turn into a bird?" Alliq asked in a quiet voice.

The snow bunting flew off instantly and began to fly around the bound children. It zipped around them, faster and faster. Eventually, it was moving so fast that the children could no longer see the bird. All they could see were streaks of colour passing in front of their eyes.

Then the little bird began to sing:

> "I will loosen the knots
> that bind you together.
> I will slacken the belt,
> so it feels like a feather."

The song was magic. The belt that had held the children together so tightly became slack, and the knots slipped open. The children wasted no time. Kunaju, Alliq, and Makpalu threw off the leather belt and began to run as fast as they could back towards their village.

Within her messy lair, the amautalik was unaware that the children had escaped. The ogress was searching for her lost tools. There were pieces of bone, rock, and animal hide everywhere. In frustration, she kicked over a large pile of bones and threw rancid animal hides around the lair in the hunt for her ulu. By the time the amautalik found her ulu and crawled back out of the hole, the children were nowhere to be seen.

Realizing that the children had escaped, the amautalik roared, "Where are my qa'tava? Where are my qa'tava?"

The magic snow bunting was still flying around the amautalik's lair. The little bird knew that the children were not safely home yet. So, it tried to distract the ogress by circling around her head. Then the little snow bunting chanted a song:

> "This timc, it sccms, you failcd to hold on to your childrcn, chirp-chirp.
> This time, it seems, you failed to hold on to your children,
> chirp-chirp."

The amautalik was outraged. The bleached bones around her lair were a testament to the fact that no one had ever escaped from her before. The ogress snarled loudly, "Small creature—no bigger than a fingernail—it is dangerous to mock me!"

"Chirp-chirp-chirp-chiiirrrrp!" The snow bunting's chirping sounded like laughter to the furious ogress.

"AAAAAHHHHHHH!" the amautalik screamed. Losing her food and then being insulted by a little snow bunting was more than she could handle. She was so mad that she could not think clearly. Had she run towards the village, she could have easily caught up with the children. Instead, the furious ogress began to jump and swat at the snow bunting.

The little bird dodged and ducked and remained just out of the amautalik's reach. No matter how hard the ogress tried, she could not catch the little bird.

Finally, after hours of jumping and swatting and lunging at the little bird, the amautalik collapsed. Out of breath and exhausted, the amautalik looked up towards the magical bird and pleaded, "Leave me, small thing. You win."

With that, the little snow bunting took off towards the children, who were now safely in the village. The magic snow bunting flew at such speed that in a few seconds it was above the children. It circled the crowd that had gathered, then flew straight to Kunaju and

landed on her hand. Alliq and Makpalu were in the process of telling the adults what had happened. Everyone in the village was listening so carefully to the boys that no one noticed the small magical bird perched on Kunaju's hand. Kunaju looked down at the bird that had helped them escape.

"Thank you, little bird," Kunaju whispered.

The bird looked up at Kunaju and nodded. Then the little snow bunting started to twitch and slowly transformed back into the old amulet made of feathers and sinew. With everyone still engrossed in the story, Kunaju carefully bent down and hid the amulet in her *kamik*.🐦

Just as the two boys were about to finish their story about their escape from the amautalik, Enooti,🐦 one of the smaller children of the village, interrupted them.

"What's that horrible smell?"

"I'm not finished!" Alliq shouted. He was irritated that the smaller boy had interrupted him in front of everyone. But before Alliq could get back to his story, a little girl made an interesting observation. "Ummm, I think there's something crawling in your hair."

Confused, Alliq ran his finger through his hair and knocked three huge insects to the ground. The crowd of people froze and then fell completely silent. Everyone stared at the giant bugs scurrying to get away.

Suddenly there was chaos in the village. "AAAAAHHHH! Giant bugs!" yelled one boy.

🐦 *Kamik*: A sealskin boot. Pronounced "kam-ik."

🐦 Enooti: Pronounced "ee-noo-tee."

"They are covered with giant lice!" shrieked a little girl.

"And they stink really bad!" yelled two children in unison.

To Alliq and Makpalu, it seemed like everyone in the village was pointing at them. The crowd quickly moved away from the children. No one would get close to the three stinky survivors who were infested with bugs.

Eventually, a tent was set up for the three children. It was away from the other dwellings and downwind from the village. The children were to stay there until the smell had worn off and the bugs were gone. Alliq and Makpalu complained constantly about being kept away from their family and friends, but as Kunaju reminded them, "It's better than being eaten by that ogress."

The two boys agreed.

After a week of staying in a tent by themselves (and three baths a day), Alliq, Makpalu, and Kunaju were free of bugs and smelled good enough to move back home.

As they were leaving the tent, Makpalu turned to Kunaju. Makpalu cleared his throat, took a deep breath, and then began,

"Umm, Kunaju . . . umm, thanks for saving us. If it wasn't for you, we probably wouldn't have gotten away."

"Yeah, and if we weren't teasing you, we might not have been caught by that monster," Alliq mumbled. Makpalu nodded his head in agreement.

"Sorry."

Kunaju just smiled. She knew the two boys were sorry for teasing her, but she never expected them to apologize. She gave them each a hug, and the three children started back towards the village.

As they walked, Kunaju slid her hand over her chest. She could feel the hard lump of the ancient amulet under her jacket. Kunaju was comforted by the thought that the amulet was safely around her neck and ready to protect her in her next adventure. The thought of another adventure made Kunaju smile.

And that is how a little girl saved her friends and herself by listening to her mother and calling on old magic that had been passed down from her ancestors.

The Amautalik
& the Orphan

Once, long ago, an amautalik was travelling across the tundra looking for children to eat. The ogress had been walking for many days and had become quite hungry. All the children she had seen were close to their watchful parents. She longed to find children who had disobeyed their parents and wandered too far from their village. Such careless children could easily be snatched without anyone noticing. But all the children in this area seemed to be well-behaved.

The ogress was almost ready to give up her hunt. Her legs were aching and her huge belly grumbled loudly. Her mind was now occupied with thoughts of eating the rotting fish and spoiled meat buried close to her underground lair. Just as she was about to turn around and head home, she spotted a little boy and a little girl sitting alone on a large rock. To her

surprise, no adults were watching over them.

The little boy, Aviuq, was an orphan. His parents had passed away when he was very young, and his grandmother had raised him. The other children in the village often teased Aviuq because he had no parents to protect him. Aviuq was used to the bullying of the other children. They threw rocks at him, called him cruel names, and did not let him play any of their games. No one even took the time to make the small orphan any warm clothing to wear.

Aviuq: Pronounced "a-vee-yok."

Instead, they gave him old clothes, which usually had holes in them and did not fit well. His pitiful kamiks were so tattered that one of his big toes had worn through the boot and was sticking out.

The little girl sitting on the rock with Aviuq was Nilak.꙳ She was the only child in the village who was kind to Aviuq. The two children were the best of friends. Nilak liked spending time with Aviuq because he was so thoughtful and smart. Aviuq had spent many nights sitting in his grandmother's tent listening to the elders telling stories. He had learned a lot from their tales and shared his knowledge with Nilak. The two friends often sat by themselves near the beach, away from the other children. Aviuq would tell Nilak the stories he had heard from elders. These friends had spent many sunny afternoons sharing stories, laughing, and watching the tide come in and go out.

On this particular day, Aviuq was telling Nilak one of his favourite stories. It was about Kiviuq, the brave adventurer who survived many dangerous obstacles during his travels. Aviuq and Nilak were so excited by the story that neither of them noticed the amautalik as she quietly crept towards them.

The stalking ogress moved carefully. As she crept closer, the ogress placed each foot gently on the ground, so as not to make a sound.

꙳ Nilak: Pronounced "nee-lak."

On and on the ogress crept, until she was directly behind the two children. She was now close enough to smell the sweat and dirt on their skin. She knew they could not escape. With great confidence, the amautalik raised her huge body up and readied herself to grab the delicious-smelling children.

As the amautalik stood up, a huge shadow fell over Aviuq and Nilak. Puzzled, they looked back to see what had caused this strange darkness. As the children's eyes met the amautalik's eyes, the ancient ogress smiled a big, menacing smile. The amautalik's open mouth dripped with saliva and was full of yellow teeth.

The ogress was massive. Her shoulders were wide and her hair was wiry and long. Aviuq thought he saw huge bugs crawling around in her hair. Her giant hands creaked as she extended her fingers and prepared to grab the children.

The two children were terrified. Nilak thought that surely they would be killed and eaten by this monster. Aviuq, however, had lived much of his life without help from others. His hardships had taught him to think for himself. He swallowed his fear and smiled bravely at the giant woman while he thought of a plan.

Carefully, Aviuq reached over to Nilak and squeezed her hand to calm her. Then, Aviuq began to move his exposed toe back and forth.

"Sssshhhh," Aviuq whispered as he pressed a finger to his lips. With his other hand, Aviuq slowly pointed to his moving toe. The puzzled amautalik looked down at the wiggling digit that peeked out of Aviuq's kamik.

"What is that in your kamik?" demanded the amautalik.

The little boy smiled at the ogress, but he did not answer right away. Instead, he continued to move his toe back and forth.

Then, Aviuq whispered, "Sssshhhh! You are going to wake it, and then it will be angry."

"What . . . what is that thing coming out of your kamik?" the amautalik asked again, with a lot less authority in her voice.

"It is a monster," whispered the boy as he stared bravely into the amautalik's eyes.

Aviuq could see the creature's smile fading, as deep creases appeared on her forehead.

The ogress swallowed hard and slowly asked, "What does the monster eat?"

"OGRESSES!" shouted Aviuq. "THIS MONSTER EATS OGRESSES!"

"KEEP HOLD OF IT! Please, keep it away from me!" howled the amautalik. And with that, the huge ogress quickly turned and sprinted away.

Confused? Aviuq had heard that this woman was very old . . . like the land itself. He guessed that the amautalik was not accustomed to a child looking bravely at her. As well, he thought that, on account of her large size, she might have not seen her own toes in many, many years.

He was right on both counts.

And that is the story of how a quick-thinking orphan outsmarted one of the most feared land spirits in the Arctic.

Other Ogres & Ogresses

The amautalik is not the only being you need to watch out for when travelling in the Arctic. The North is filled with many strange and dangerous beings and creatures. Depending on where you travel, you risk encountering hulking ogres and ogresses, enormous giants, vicious trolls, and creatures of all shapes and sizes.

   The following pages will introduce you to several of these beings. This is only a glimpse, mind you, as there are too many to list here.

AKLAJUK

Pronounced "ak-la-yook"

Aklajuk is a powerful grizzly bear spirit. To some he appears as a huge grizzly bear, and to others he looks like a huge ogre with large claws and teeth.

He is known to rob graves and food caches. He and his kind are feared, as they are powerful, fast, and always on the lookout for things to eat.

AASIVAK Pronounced "aa-see-vak"

Aasivak is actually an ancient spider that possesses the magical ability to assume a human-like form.

Travellers should be cautious of any strange dwelling they might encounter in their journeys on the land. Like the web of a spider, once you have entered Aasivak's home it is very difficult to escape.

NAHAINGAJAAQ

Pronounced "na-hang-a-yuk"

This huge ogress wanders the western Arctic of Canada. Nahaingajaaq is a cannibal, and she is always on the lookout for lone travellers. You can recognize her by her large size, and her tattooed and bone-pierced face. She is known to carry an adze and a large ulu, as these are her weapons.

NARAJAT
Pronounced "nar-a-yat"

Narajat is an ogre with an enormous appetite. It is said that he can eat several adult caribou in one sitting. Narajat's most distinguishing feature (other than his huge size and ogre-like appearance) is his huge belly.

When hunting, Narajat must lash his belly with strips of leather so it doesn't get in his way.